Uncle Blubbafink's

seriously

ridiculous

stories

by Keith graves

SCHOLASTIC PRESS · NEW YORK

To **MOM** and **DAD**

Copyright © 2001 by Keith Graves

All rights reserved. Published by Scholastic Press, a division of Scholastic Inc.,
Publishers since 1920. SCHOLASTIC and SCHOLASTIC PRESS and associated logos are
trademarks and/or registered trademarks of Scholastic Inc. No part of this publication
may be reproduced, or stored in a retrieval system, or transmitted in any form or by any
means, electronic, mechanical, photocopying, recording, or otherwise, without written permission of the publisher. For information regarding permission, write to Scholastic Inc.,
Attention: Permissions Department, 555 Broadway, New York, NY 10012.

Library of Congress Cataloging-in-Publication Data
Graves, Keith.
Uncle Blubbafink's seriously ridiculous stories / written and illustrated by Keith Graves.—1st ed.
p. cm.
Contents: Abraham Sandwich and George Washing Machine—The legend of Smoky the
volcano—The dragon whose head was a station wagon—The history of cows.
ISBN 0-439-24083-2
1. Tall tales. 2. Children's stories, American. [1. Tall tales. 2. Short stories.] I. Title.
PZ7.G77524 Un 2001   [Fic]—dc21   00-047030
10 9 8 7 6 5 4 3 2 1   01 02 03 04 05
Printed in Mexico   49
First edition, September 2001
The text type was set in 16-point Bodoni Bold.
The artwork for this book was rendered in
acrylic paint on illustration board.
Book design by Kristina
Albertson

howdy.

OK, so I'm Uncle Blubbafink.

Hello already. I hear you're looking for a good story or two. **Well, you came to the right place.** You want stories? I'll give you stories. **Millions of 'em. True stories, mind you, not any of that fairy godmother hoo-ha. Actual historical events witnessed with my own eyes.** Like the one about my old pal Abraham Sandwich. *We used to surf together back in '67. . . .*

Abraham Sandwich and George Washing Machine

It was about fourscore and seven years ago,

give or take a score, when my old pal Abraham Sandwich moved to Miami. He built a nice log cabin right on the beach. Abe was a big fellow. He ate **ham** sandwiches like they were going out of style. But Abe was some surfer. Best three-hundred-pound surfer in Florida.

George Washing Machine lived next door to Honest **Ham**. George was a funny little guy who looked like a washing machine with skinny legs. And he had a thing about chopping down cherry trees. If George saw a cherry tree, **BAM**! He'd chop it down. That's the kinda guy he was.

Well, one day Abe and I are out surfing and we're having so much fun we forget to eat lunch.

So Abe says, "I'm so hungry I could eat twelve **ham** sandwiches! Well, maybe not twelve exactly, but at least nine. Yeah, nine for sure." Honest **Ham** was a really honest guy, see.

I said, "**Ham** is good. I could eat **ham**."

We went home and opened his fridge. No **ham**. We looked in his backyard. All his **ham** trees were cut down.

In a panic, Honest  ran next door.

"Hey, George! George Washing Machine!

Have you seen my **ham**?

And **who** chopped down my **ham** orchard?"

"Oh, wow," said George. "Were those **ham** trees? I could have *sworn* they were cherry trees. I just couldn't resist them. I saw them sitting there and **BAM**! I chopped them down. I guess that's the kinda guy I am. Anyway, after all that chopping, I was hungry and there was a lovely **ham** in your fridge. By the way, you're out of pickles."

Abe was very upset at this point.

"You chopped down my **ham** trees, you crazy washing machine! Do you understand what this means? I have no **HAM**! I'm **HAM**-LESS! And I'm **STARVED**."

"Gee, Abe, you guys can have dinner with me," offered George. "I have some clams and some yams. **We'll have a feast!**"

Abe said, "Truth is, clams make my feet swell, but I'll try the yams."

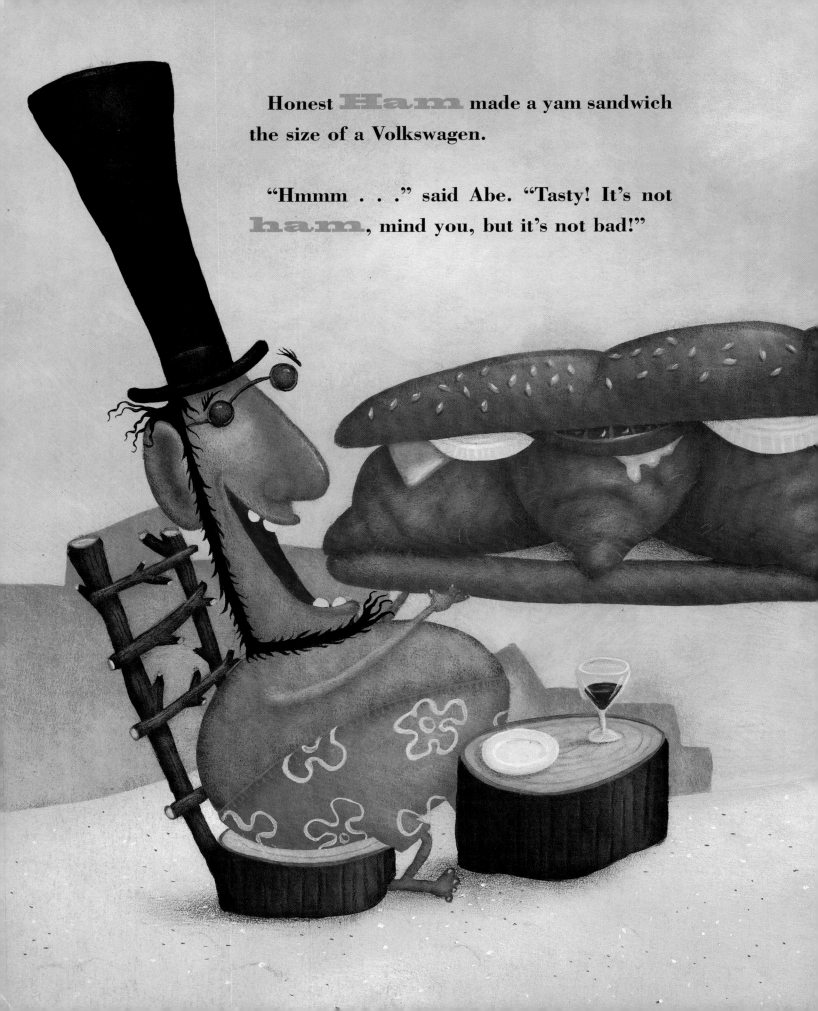

Honest **Ham** made a yam sandwich the size of a Volkswagen.

"Hmmm . . ." said Abe. "Tasty! It's not **ham**, mind you, but it's not bad!"

And he ate the whole thing. Then he ate another, and another, and another. He loved the yams. In fact, Abe won't even look at a ham these days. Now all the surfers call him Honest Abra "YAM" Sandwich.

yam, get it?

the Legend of Smoky the Volcano

One day, while walking in the jungle,

I heard a sad whimpering sound. There at my feet was a tiny volcano. "Hey, pal, did you fall out of your nest, or what?" I said. As all us science types know, once a volcano pup falls out of its nest, the mother volcano abandons it. So I named him Smoky, gave him my socks, and fed him some trail mix.

bok!

bok
bok

bok!

bok
bok

bok

bok!

Next thing I know, the little guy's following me around like my shadow. So I started thinking . . . I know a family of lonely **chickens** who could give him a nice home. Sure enough, they loved him. They taught him to play **chicken** games, sing **chicken** songs, walk that goofy **chicken** walk, and they fed him lots and lots of homemade worm pies. Smoky was happy as a clam.

Then he started growing.
Mama **Chicken** called me up
and said, "We love Smoky,
but he eats too much. He's
gigantic! And he's
making very weird sounds."

"He's not rumbling,
is he?" I said.

"Yes!" she cried.

"And shaking?"

"Yes! Yes!"

"And there wouldn't be
smoke coming out of his
ears?"

"Yes! Yes! Yes!"

bok!

There was only one thing to do. The chickens and I took Smoky back to his natural habitat and set him free. The only thing sadder than a crying volcano is a crying chicken. But everything worked out well.

Smoky found a nice spot to settle down and
then erupted like a Roman candle for about two weeks.

He created his own island!

Now the **chickens** vacation
on the Island of Smoke-ahoa-loa every
year and bring Smoky homemade worm pies.
I prefer cherry pie myself. But then, I'm not a volcano.

eat, eat.
You look thin.

the Dragon whose Head was a Station Wagon

Dave was your basic dragon:

blue skin, bad breath, big feet. . . . You know the type.

Now, Dave was trying to lose a couple of pounds so he was on a strict no-*princess* diet. He had just eaten a nice low-fat meal of roasted auto parts when he became very sleepy.

So he turned in early.

The next morning, Dave noticed something strange. His head had become a station wagon while he was asleep. His head had never become a vehicle before. **"Oh, no!"** yelled Dave. **"My chin is like tin! My head feels like lead!** My ears are full of gears! I can't let anyone see me like this! I need a disguise."

Yuck.

So Dave put on a hat and a phony beard. *I hope no one recognizes me*, he thought, as he walked down the street to terrorize his favorite castle.

I was the resident knight in this particular castle, and I happened to see him coming. "**Whoa!** Who are you? You're about the ugliest dragon I've ever seen!"

"Well," said Dave, "I'm new in town and I was wondering if you would like to come out and try to slay me. Or maybe I could steal your *princess*, although I'm on a no-*princess* diet. They're fattening, you know."

"Yeah, sure, you betcha," I said. "Dave is my usual dragon, but since he's not around, I'd be happy to slay you."

So I **zinged** a few arrows at the ugly dragon.

"**Ha!**" roared Dave. "**I'll barbecue you like a pork chop!**" And a huge flame shot out of his carburetor, setting his beard on fire. Then his hat fell off.

"Hey, wait a minute," I said.
"Now I recognize you.
You're *Dave the dragon*!
And your head is a station wagon!
**Ha! That's the
funniest thing
I've ever seen!"**

"You're so funny you should be on TV."
"You think so?" asked Dave.
"Would I kid you?" I said.

So I got him a job doing the weather on Channel Three.
Best thing on TV, I tell ya.
True story, too.
True as toenails.

the History of Cows

moo

Cows. They're so weird.

They're always eating grass and standing around in the rain. And what's the deal with "**moo**," anyway? **Moo, moo, moo.** That's all they ever talk about.

Well, I'll tell you a secret. Cows come from the moon. That's why they're so strange.

See, in the old days, when I was a young tyke, there weren't any cows on Earth. We had no chocolate milk, no cheesecake, no ice cream. Life was tough without cows.

All the cows were way up there on the MOON.
Of course, the MOON was green back then because it
was all covered with grass. It was cow heaven, I tell ya.
I'd lie awake at night listening to them munching and mumbling.

Well, time went by and pretty soon those cows ate every last blade of grass on the entire moon.

Boy, did they start a ruckus then! You have never heard such a racket as a MOON full of hungry cows complaining about how the grass is all gone. We couldn't get any sleep with all that noise every night when the MOON came up.

Something had to be done.

So I drove my rocket ship up there and loaded up those loud-mouthed bovines. Boy! Was that a stinky ride home!

P-U!

Anyway, I got them back down to Earth all safe and sound and made a deal with them.

They got to eat all the grass they wanted in exchange for giving us lots of milk shakes and **Swiss cheese**.

But those cows still get homesick from time to time. You can hear 'em to this day saying,

"MoooooooN . . . MOooooooon."

That's true, about the cows. Hey, would I make that up? Of course not. Not your old Uncle Blub. I like you too much.

Now get outta here already.

UNCLE BLUBBAFINK

gratefully

✖ **acknowledges** the **following people, places,** *and things:*

The Yam Growers of America, The Ham Growers of America, The Cheap-Chopper Chainsaw Co., Freddy's Surf Boards, The Bovine Historical Society, NASA for their technical support in reaching the moon, The moon, Lunar Cheese Shoppe, The Outreach Program for Wayward Volcanoes, The Professional Chickens' Union, The Henny Penny Dance Company, Aunt Bessie's Favorite Worm Pies, Inc., The Toledo Fire Department for their invaluable help with dragon-related fires, Ed's Used Station Wagons, Dr. Inferno's Smooth Shave for Dragons, MidTown Princess Rental, The Mayor of Miami, Bob Dylan, The Hair Goo Corporation for creating my lovely coif, The guy on the bus this morning who told me where to get off, and finally, My analyst for suggesting I tell my crazy stories to someone else for a change.

☞ No animals were injured in the making of this book, although I did get a little tennis elbow from all that archery with the dragon.